HIGH SCHOOL MUSICAL

THE ESSENTIAL GUIDE

Written by
Catherine Saunders

CONTENTS

New Year's Eve

When Troy Bolton and Gabriella Montez meet at a ski resort on New Year's Eve, it marks the beginning of an amazing journey for both of them. Reluctantly finding themselves at the Teen Party, Troy and Gabriella somehow end up singing karaoke together. They discover that their voices match perfectly and end up having a great time! Could this be the start of something?

Troy would prefer to be practicing his jump shots, while Gabriella would rather be reading her book, but fortunately their parents have other ideas...

Although Gabriella has sung in her church choir, she has always been too nervous to sing solo, while Troy has only ever sung in the shower!

After their song, Troy and Gabriella swap cell phone numbers, but they doubt that they will ever see each other again.

EAST HIGH

New student Gabriella Montez is excited about making a fresh start at East High.

Welcome to East High! Run by the laidback Principal Matsui, it's a friendly school where the students work hard and play hard too. The school prides itself on its broad range of extracurricular activities, from sports and music, to arts and crafts. Come take a closer look at East High.

Student Body

There's a place for everyone at East High—science dudes, sports nuts, musical geniuses, and math maestros. But once a student has found their place, they usually stick with that clique. No one messes with the status quo!

Ms. Popular

Everyone at East High knows Sharpay Evans and no one dares get in her way. Unfortunately, new girl Gabriella Montez has no idea...

Cafeteria

The cafeteria is not just a place to eat lunch, it is THE spot to catch up on all the latest gossip. When Troy Bolton wants to try out for the school musical, it is the talk of the cafeteria!

School Spirit

East High students are proud of their school and always support school teams, whether it's cheering on the Wildcats basketball team or getting behind the brainy Scholastic Decathletes. Go East High!

School Days

East High is a great school, but even the brainiacs can't help counting the days, weeks, and hours until it is vacation time again!

WHO'S WHO

At East High, the students have formed cliques. From sports fans to brainiacs, drama geeks to skater dudes, these groups study together, lunch together, and hang out together. And they NEVER mix because the golden rule is "stick with what you know." But the arrival of new girl Gabriella Montez shakes up East High's status quo, forever.

Brainiacs

The brainiacs are A+ overachievers who spend hours and hours in the library, do their homework on time, and love taking on extra-credit assignments.

Drama Club

Sharpay Evans
The Drama Club's leading lady has been a star since kindergarten!

Ryan Evans
Ryan has starred with his twin sister in every school production.

Kelsi Nielsen
Musician Kelsi is excited when her composition is chosen for the school musical.

School Band

The East High Marching Band practice three times a week and go to Band Camp every summer with other local schools.

The Wildcats

The East High basketball team is nicknamed the Wildcats. The guys on the team always hang out together, discussing tactics or just shooting hoops in the backyard of their captain, Troy Bolton.

Cheerleaders

No high school would be complete without a cheerleading squad. Their athletic routines and rousing cheers help the Wildcats to up their game on the basketball court.

Teachers

Ms. Darbus

The drama teacher doesn't think sports are as important as the theater!

Coach Bolton

The Wildcats' coach thinks practice is more important than detention.

Other Cliques

Skater Dudes   Math Club
Gardening Club   Scuba Club
Science Club   Hockey Club
Cooking Club   Art Club

THE PLAYMAKER

Troy Bolton is captain of the East High Wildcats basketball team and one of the most popular guys in school. While his teammates and fellow students look up to him, Troy sees himself simply as the playmaker—the one who makes everyone else look good.

Troy is a modest, unassuming kind of guy. He doesn't judge people and is friends with everyone.

Team Player

Wearing his trademark #14 jersey, Troy has turned in some state-championship winning performances for the Wildcats. However, his teammates voted him captain because he is the kind of guy who always does the right thing.

Instant Connection

Ever since Troy and Gabriella met on New Year's Eve, they have felt like old friends.

Troy sometimes feels that his Dad has mapped his whole future out for him. The question is: What does Troy really want?

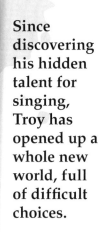

Since discovering his hidden talent for singing, Troy has opened up a whole new world, full of difficult choices.

Did you know?

★ Troy has two secret hangouts—the Gardening Club's rooftop garden and the treehouse in his backyard.

★ Troy also loves snowboarding and playing golf.

The Basketball Guy

Troy is the Wildcats' captain, their star player, and the coach's son. Until he meets Gabriella, Troy has never wanted to do anything except play basketball. However, these days he thinks that there might be more to him than just being "the basketball guy."

Troy's casual style reflects his laidback attitude to life. However, he scrubs up well for important dates such as the Prom.

"The world looks different to me than before."

MATH GIRL

Gabriella Montez transfers schools nearly every year because of her Mom's job. However, when she moves to East High and sees a familiar face in homeroom, Gabriella begins to hope that she might be able to stay around a little longer this time.

Gabriella has a close relationship with her Mom. Mrs Montez is proud of her smart daughter, but she just wants her to be happy.

Settling In

Gabriella can't believe that she has ended up at the same school as Troy Bolton! She would love to sing with him again.

Gabriella makes lots of new friends at East High. Taylor McKessie gives her the heads up on who's who and is delighted when she learns that Gabriella is a math genius!

Secret's Out!

At her previous schools, Gabriella has always been labelled a "freaky math girl," but she hopes that moving to East High will be a new start for her. However, when Sharpay Evans learns the truth, she wastes no time in letting the whole world in on Gabriella's little secret...

Did you know?

 Singing and math are not Gabriella's only talents—she is also first-aid certified and a strong swimmer.

Gabriella is sweet and kind. She believes in Ryan and encourages him to share his dancing skills with the Wildcats.

Gabriella's style is fresh and feminine. She likes floral prints, bright colors, and has an amazing shoe collection!

"It's cool coming here and being... anyone I want to be."

Making A Difference

When she arrives, Gabriella has no idea of the changes she will bring to East High. She inspires Troy to follow his heart and find his voice, and challenges those around her to work together, no matter who they are.

SCHOOL STAR

Sharpay Evans is the undisputed Queen of East High. She has been the star of no less than seventeen school drama productions and is not used to any competition. In Sharpay's opinion there's only room for one star, and that's her!

Sharpay is a total Daddy's girl and used to getting what she wants. When Sharpay Evans speaks, people usually do what she says!

Miss Popular

Sharpay just loves being the center of attention. Many of the East High students feel starstruck around her, asking her for autographs and treating her like a celebrity. Even Wildcat Zeke Baylor has a not-so-secret crush on Sharpay.

Double Trouble

Sharpay's song and dance partner is her twin brother, Ryan. She relies on him to help her get what she wants.

Showing Off

For Sharpay performance is everything—fabulous costumes, great choreography, and a showstopping song.

"It's pretty obvious that I'm special."

Did you know?

Sharpay's favorite color is pink. She has a pink car, a pink bedroom, and even personalized pink golf balls!

Sharpay used to be a Girl Scout and she won "most innovative hairdo" badges three times.

Simply Fabulous!

Sharpay likes everything to be fabulous. Why shouldn't she be the star of the show, the most popular girl in school, and have Troy Bolton by her side? But somehow things never quite work out the way she hopes...

Every girl needs a best friend and Sharpay's is her cute little dog, Waffles.

From glitter and sparkles, to bright colors and over-the-top accessories, Sharpay likes to be noticed!

GOTTA DANCE!

Like his twin sister, Sharpay, Ryan Evans was born to perform, and at first he doesn't welcome competition from Troy and Gabriella. But Ryan is a good guy and he soon discovers that it is more fun working with the Wildcats, than against them.

While Sharpay is an old-fashioned Daddy's girl, Ryan enjoys practicing yoga with his Mom.

Talented Twins

Ryan is a talented singer, dancer, and choreographer. But will anyone ever notice him next to the dazzling Sharpay?

Ryan loves creating high-energy routines for himself and Sharpay, and he soon turns his talents to working with Kelsi and the Wildcats.

"Oh well, that's showbiz!"

Hidden Talents

During the summer vacation at Lava Springs Country Club, Ryan reveals a hidden talent for baseball. More importantly, he learns that it feels great to be part of a team.

Did you know?

★ Ryan can also play the ukelele.

★ Ryan's Mom has a cute nickname for him— "Pumpkin."

Ryan's clothes reflect his outgoing personality. He likes bold colors and patterns and is rarely seen without his trademark hat.

Star In His Eyes

Sharpay is usually the dominant twin, with Ryan happy to follow her lead. But when Ryan becomes closer to the Wildcats, he learns to follow his own path and finally steps out from his sister's shadow.

Gabriella knows how it feels to be the new person. She helps Ryan to show the Wildcats what kind of a guy he really is.

SPORTS CRAZY

Chad Danforth lives for sports, especially basketball. At first he can't understand what his buddy Troy is doing messing around with the Drama Club. However, when Chad realizes that Troy is serious about singing he pulls out all the stops to support his teammate.

Chad is always full of energy and up for anything. He can usually be relied upon to come up with a smart wisecrack, even if it is just the message on his T-shirt!

Best Friend

Chad has been friends with Troy Bolton since preschool. They are as close as brothers, which means that they sometimes fight, but always make up again.

On the basketball court, Chad is Troy's deputy. Off court, he is Troy's main man and watches his buddy's back at all times.

While Troy discovers his talent for drama, Chad makes new friends, including brainiac Taylor McKessie.

"I've been behind on homework since preschool."

Did you know?

⭐ **Chad is saving up to buy a car.**

⭐ **Chad would really like to take Taylor McKessie to the Senior Prom.**

Chad's second favorite sport is baseball, but forget dancing—that's a whole new ballgame!

Chad has a casual look and usually sports a funky T-shirt.

Hoops Dude

Chad thinks about sports 24/7. Basketball is his first love and he usually carries a ball with him, just in case he wants to shoot a few hoops.

When Ryan proves that he can play baseball, Chad realizes that he might be able to "do dance" after all.

NATURAL LEADER

Taylor McKessie is a natural born overachiever. She is leader of East High's science club, a member of the Scholastic Decathlon team, and class President. Taylor used to think that sports and drama were a waste of time, but since she started hanging out with the Wildcats, Taylor has learned that academic success is not the only important thing in her life.

Taylor is so smart that she even memorizes the lunch menu in the school cafeteria!

Who's The Boss?

During summer vacation, Taylor puts her organizational skills to the test as Activities' Coordinator at the Lava Springs Country Club.

Coordinating all the guests and staff at the Lava Springs Midsummer's Talent Show is no problem for the super-efficient, always-on-her-game Taylor.

Good Friend

Taylor and Gabriella have more than just brains in common. They enjoy hanging out, and Taylor is always ready to give Gabriella honest advice.

"Wake up, sister!"

Did you know?

★ Taylor's ambition is to be President of the USA.

★ Taylor's older sister has ten rules about boy behavior, which Taylor passes on to Gabriella.

Taylor develops a close friendship with Wildcat Chad Danforth. His boyish charm brings out her sweet and caring side!

Taylor likes to mix smart, preppy style with bold colors and strong patterns. Her look means business!

Taking Charge
Taylor is confident, calm, and in control. Super-organized and practical, she never lets her friends and fellow students down.

SHY GENIUS

Kelsi Nielsen is a talented musician and composer. She is naturally shy and quiet, except when it comes to music. When her original creation *Twinkle Towne* is chosen as the East High Spring Musical, it opens up a whole new world for Kelsi.

Kelsi has a key to the East High music room and goes there before class every day so that she can practice piano.

Kelsi's head is full of music. She spends most of her free time composing new songs, and dreams of studying music at the Juilliard School in New York.

Finding Inspiration

Troy and Gabriella help Kelsi to believe in her talent, while Kelsi helps them to find the music in each other. Troy and Gabriella's passion for singing inspires Kelsi to write songs especially for them.

"You're the playmaker here, Kelsi."

Kelsi and Sharpay don't share the same musical tastes, but Kelsi learns to stand up for herself and make sure that her songs are performed just the way she wrote them.

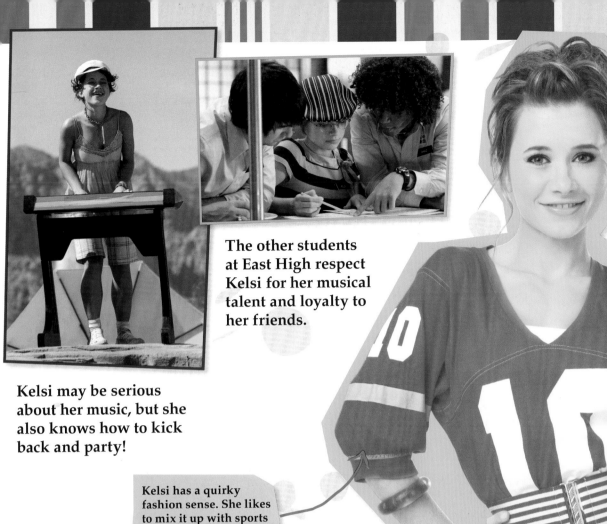

The other students at East High respect Kelsi for her musical talent and loyalty to her friends.

Kelsi may be serious about her music, but she also knows how to kick back and party!

Kelsi has a quirky fashion sense. She likes to mix it up with sports chic, retro plaids, and cute accessories.

Did you know?

When the Wildcats win the State Championship, Troy gives Kelsi the game ball.

Walking Tall

Since the success of *Twinkle Towne*, Kelsi has made lots of new friends and grown into a confident young woman. During the senior year, she becomes close friends with Ryan. They share a passion for music and fabulous hats!

TEAM PLAYERS

East High is full of amazingly talented students, from brainiacs to b-ballers, cheerleaders to chefs, singers to skaters. Come and meet three of Troy and Gabriella's best buddies and discover their secret talents, best moments, and favorite things.

Zeke Baylor

Secret Chef

Zeke is a basketball dude at heart, but his friends can't get enough of his delicious cakes and cookies!

When Troy admits that he likes singing, Zeke confesses that he too has a secret passion—baking.

Ms. Darbus doesn't always appreciate Zeke's laidback and chatty personality...

Dream Girl

Zeke admires Sharpay Evans from afar. First his mouthwatering muffins get her attention, and later she informs him that he will be her date for the Senior Prom. Zeke can't wait!

Jason Cross

Nice Guy

Jason is one of life's good guys. But when he asks Ms. Darbus about her favorite summer memory, moments before school lets out for summer vacation, the rest of the class can't believe it!

Everyone loves sweet and dependable Jason. He is a loyal Wildcat and a good friend.

Martha Cox

Bopping Brainiac

The other students at East High may not realize it but Martha is far more then just a science dude.

Martha has always been known as a brainiac, but she too has a secret hobby—she loves dancing to hip-hop!

Martha becomes good friends with Gabriella, Taylor, Kelsi, and the rest of the Wildcats.

WHAT TEAM?

The crowd gives the Wildcats great support. During a game, Troy always searches for a special face in the crowd who will inspire him to play better.

Wildcats! What team? Wildcats! Get'cha head in the game! Led by their captain, Troy Bolton, the East High Wildcats are a tight-knit team. In recent seasons they have established a winning record against their local rivals, the West High Knights.

"Win together, lose together... teammates."

Gameplan

Coach Bolton and the Wildcats spend a lot of time working out different plays to fool the opposition. However, they also have a secret weapon— their lucky socks! When the Wildcats are on a winning streak, they never, ever wash their socks.

Did you know?

The team have a lucky mascot named Wildcat. No one knows who is actually inside the costume, although Ryan Evans dons the suit during the Wildcats' last ever game.

Proud Dad

Coach Bolton himself was a Wildcat in the class of 1981. He is proud of Troy's achievements and would love his son to continue following in his footsteps and play basketball for the University of Albuquerque Redhawks.

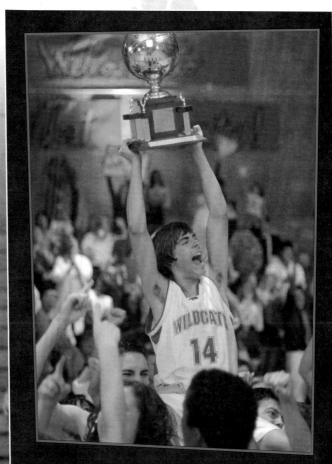

Champions!

Troy loves the feeling of winning at basketball. Trouble is he loves singing, too. If only there was a way for this Wildcat to play ball and do drama...

TWINKLE TOWNE

For the first time ever, Drama Club stars Sharpay and Ryan have rivals for the lead roles.

With music and lyrics by the talented Kelsi Nielsen, *Twinkle Towne* is East High's must-see winter musical. The Drama Club always puts on a fabulous show, but this time there may be a few suprises...

Auditions

At first the auditions for *Twinkle Towne* follow a familiar pattern, as Sharpay and Ryan perform an up-tempo version of Kelsi's song, "What I've Been Looking For." Sharpay and Ryan are confident that the roles are theirs, but two nervous latecomers look set to steal the show!

When Ms. Darbus hears Troy and Gabriella sing, she realizes that they have real talent and gives them a callback.

Ms. Darbus says that Troy and Gabriella are too late to audition. Disappointed, they are about to give up, until Kelsi drops her sheet music. As they rush to help her, she offers to show them how her song should have sounded.

As Kelsi plays "What I've Been Looking For" to Troy and Gabriella, they join in the song.

28

Did you know?

★ **Ms. Darbus's favorite summer memory is from 1988, the year she took part in the Ashland Shakespeare Festival in Oregon.**

Sharpay loves being the star of the show and she will do everything that she can to make sure that she wins the lead role in *Twinkle Towne*, not Gabriella.

Callbacks

Sharpay and Ryan are not impressed when they discover that they are not the only pair with a callback. So, Sharpay persuades Ms. Darbus to switch the callbacks so they clash with Troy's basketball game and Gabriella's Scholastic Decathlon. Meanwhile Sharpay and Ryan perform another showstopping routine.

"The theater waits for no one."

Breaking Free

The brainiacs and Wildcats join forces to help Troy and Gabriella make the callbacks and win the lead roles. The math girl and the basketball guy show East High that it is OK to follow your heart and be different, and even Sharpay Evans wishes them good luck!

SUMMER TIME

 The Wildcats are going to have the best summer! For Gabriella it is the first summer in five years that she hasn't moved to a new town, and she can't wait to spend some time with Troy. But with college to think of, Troy, Gabriella, and the Wildcats also need summer jobs—fast!

What Time Is It?

As the last few seconds of the semester run out, the class can finally celebrate the fact that school's out and it's vacation time. Sharpay and Ryan have a fabulous summer to look forward to, relaxing at the Lava Springs Country Club. And Sharpay has a plan to get Troy Bolton there too.

"I want to remember my summer."

Located in the New Mexico desert, Lava Springs boasts a huge golf course, a state-of-the-art gym, a luxury spa, and a five-star restaurant.

Mr. and Mrs. Evans

The members only Lava Springs Country Club is owned by Sharpay and Ryan's parents—Vance and Derby Evans. While Mr. Evans commutes back and forth by helicopter, Mrs. Evans spends her time in the spa and the yoga studio.

Fun In The Sun

Sharpay plans to have the Lava Springs' manager, Mr. Fulton, offer Troy a job. However, her plan backfires when Troy brings the rest of the Wildcats with him. They plan to work hard and play hard too!

Did you know?

★ Sharpay Evans considers herself the unofficial Queen of Lava Springs. She has her own personalized lounger by the pool and a group of gal pals called the "Sharpettes."

WORK IT OUT!

Mr. Fulton
As the manager of Lava Springs, Mr. Fulton has a lot of responsibility. However, his biggest job is keeping Sharpay Evans happy!

The Wildcats soon find out that spending the summer at Lava Springs is no picnic. Mr. Fulton expects them to work hard and stick to the rules. However, Troy convinces them that if they all pull together, they can still have a great summer.

Top Jobs

Waiter/Caddy
Troy and Chad's jobs are to wait tables and caddy for the golfers.

Kitchen
Jason and Martha are put to work in the kitchen.

Chef
Zeke hopes to pick up some tips as Assistant Chef.

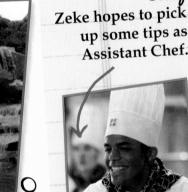

Piano Player
Kelsi's musical talents are put to good use, playing relaxing piano for guests.

"You're paid to work, not to play."

While most of the Wildcats sweat it out in the kitchen, Gabriella is given the job of lifeguard while Taylor is Activities' Coordinator.

32

Summer Stress

The Wildcats can't help noticing that Troy is being given special treatment. Chad feels like his buddy has let him down while Gabriella begins to think that she can't believe Troy's promises anymore.

Chad doesn't enjoy being a waiter, it will be worth it if he can save up enough money to buy a car.

Favorite Employee

Sharpay has big plans for Troy. She has Mr. Fulton promote him to golf pro and gives him special privileges.

As part of his new job, Troy is given new clothes, a golf cart, and honorary membership at Lava Springs. He must also give golf lessons to guests—and Sharpay.

Mr. Fulton's strict rules almost make Chad think fondly of detention with Ms. Darbus!

CHAD

PERFECT PLAN

For Sharpay it's simple math—she is the most popular girl at East High and Troy is the most popular boy so they should work together. Right? The only snag is Troy seems to prefer hanging out with Gabriella and the Wildcats! But Sharpay has a plan.

Sharpay just wants everything to to be fabulous—and that means singing with Troy!

Secret Mission

Sharpay tries to get Troy to Lava Springs for the summer, but he brings all the Wildcats with him. So Sharpay decides to keep a watchful eye on him while she plans her next move.

Under Pressure

Sharpay has it all worked out! With Mr. Fulton's help, she arranges a smart new job for Troy. She also uses her Dad's contacts to line up some amazing opportunities with the U of A Redhawks—and the rest of the Wildcats are not invited!

Did you know?

Troy's Dad has been taking him to the University of Albuquerque Redhawks' games since he was a kid. Coach Bolton would be so proud if Troy joined the U of A alumni.

When Sharpay learns that Kelsi has written a song especially for Troy and Gabriella, she has to have it. And she wants it her way!

Dream Duet

Knowing that Troy is worried about his future, Sharpay lines up some college scouts to come and watch him sing with her. As they practice a jazzed-up version of Kelsi's song, Sharpay thinks her plan has finally worked!

When Troy finally realizes that he must follow his heart and be loyal to the Wildcats, it looks like the show is over for Sharpay. Troy just hopes it's not too late to fix things with Gabriella.

"I don't want any surprises."

Although it is a duet, the new version of the song is all about Sharpay! Troy feels torn between thinking of his future and being true to the Wildcats.

STAR DAZZLE

Every year Lava Springs Country Club hosts a Midsummer's Night Talent Show. It is THE social event of the year and the winner of the Talent Show is presented with the prestigious Star Dazzle Award. For the last five years the award has been won by Sharpay Evans...

Wokring Hard

With Sharpay focused on her own plans for the show, Ryan shares his fantastic choreography ideas with the Wildcats. They have great fun working out a showstopping routine.

Sharpay cannot believe that Ryan is working with the Wildcats. She feels betrayed by her own brother!

Other Acts

Sharpay is not the only star of the Midsummer's Night Talent Show. Other acts include twinkle-toed tap dancer, Tina.

Mrs. Hoffenfeffer and her outspoken sock puppet are desperate to win the Star Dazzle Award this year.

"Everyday"

When Troy realizes that what's happening right now is more important than what might happen in the future, he tells Sharpay that he can't sing with her. Kelsi overhears him and, along with Ryan, works out a way to fix everything.

Ryan and Kelsi persuade Troy to learn a new song and then Gabriella arrives on cue for the perfect duet.

Making It Right

Sharpay might be a devious diva, but she also has a big heart. So when Mr. Fulton announces the winner of this year's Star Dazzle Award, Sharpay makes sure that it goes to the right person—her talented brother Ryan.

When Troy and Gabriella reveal their secret talents for singing, everything changes at East High.

TEAMWORK

The old cliques and groups have faded away and the students of East High have realized that they are all one big team. It's not always easy, but at least they know that they're all in this together!

"All for one, one for all."

Gabriella wanted to have the best summer ever. After a shaky start, it has turned out to be pretty great after all.

Chad and Taylor have grown closer over the summer. Maybe Chad will finally be able to pluck up the courage to ask her out?

New Friends

Ryan truly has had the best summer ever. He has made friends with the Wildcats and earned his sister's respect. And he finally has a Star Dazzle Award of his very own! He feels like a new person and can't wait to start the senior year at East High.

Zeke takes any chance he can to get close to Sharpay. Maybe one day she will realize how great he is!

Moving Forward

After a hardworking summer at Lava Springs, the Wildcats are ready to go back to school and face their senior year. They will have to make tough decisions about their future, but until then it's all for one!

Troy and Gabriella don't know what the future holds, they just want to enjoy right now.

THE FUTURE

Although Troy and Gabriella are worried about what will happen next year, they want to enjoy their senior year while they can.

As the senior year at East High begins, the Wildcats face some tough decisions. They must think about where to go to college, decide what to study, and work out how they are all going to stay friends when senior year is over.

"Not everything has to change."

Going Her Own Way

Being at East High has opened up a whole new world for Gabriella. She has made some great friends and helped bring the different cliques at East High together. She is not sure that she is ready to leave it all behind just yet.

Gabriella's Mom has always wanted her to go to Stanford University, but Stanford is 1053 miles away!

Thanks to Gabriella, Taylor has learned to relate better to her fellow students, even the jocks!

40

Music Scholarship

Ms. Darbus announces that four East High students are being considered for one scholarship to the prestigious Juilliard School in New York City—Sharpay Evans, Ryan Evans, Kelsi Nielsen, and Troy Bolton!

Sharpay thinks the scholarship is a "done deal."

Ryan would love to study dance at Juilliard.

Kelsi has always wanted to go to Juilliard.

Troy has no idea who put him up for the scholarship.

Did you know?

Gabriella has already won a place on Stanford's early acceptance program, but she doesn't know how to tell Troy...

Unlike Troy, Chad has no big worries about his future. He can't wait to start at U of A and hopes that his best buddy will be there with him. As long as he can play basketball, Chad is happy!

Difficult Decisions

Troy feels under pressure to do the right thing, trouble is he doesn't know what that is! He feels torn between basketball and wanting to find out where his newly discovered talent for singing might take him. And then there's Gabriella...

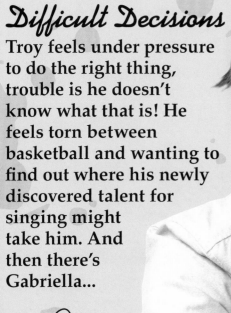

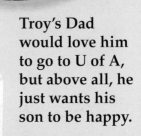

Troy's Dad would love him to go to U of A, but above all, he just wants his son to be happy.

SENIOR YEAR

When Kelsi signs the whole class up for the spring musical, they are not happy about it. Troy wants to work on his truck, Zeke wants to try out new recipes, Jason wants to study, and Taylor says she is too busy editing the yearbook. But Gabriella reminds them all that it is their last chance to do something together.

As usual, Taylor has a million and one other commitments, but she will make time for one last show at East High. Gabriella is right, the Wildcats should have fun together, while they still can.

Master Plan

Sharpay has it all figured out! She will be the star of the musical and win the scholarship to Juilliard. To make sure she gets the best songs in the show, she orders Ryan to hang out with Kelsi.

The Wildcats play their last ever game at East High. It's an emotional moment for the team, but at least now they have more time to focus on their final show. Ms. Darbus suggests the perfect theme—the challenges of senior year.

Did you know?

Although Sharpay doesn't believe him, Troy has no idea who put him forward for the Juilliard scholarship. It was Ms. Darbus!

As Ryan and Kelsi spend more time together, the shy composer and the budding choreographer discover that they have a lot in common. Ryan forgets that he is supposed to be Sharpay's spy and asks Kelsi to be his prom date!

"I think we should stage the perfect prom."

"Just Want To Be With You"

Once again, Troy and Gabriella inspire Kelsi to write the perfect song for them. But as Gabriella heads off to Stanford early, it seems like the end of the line for the show, and for the Wildcats.

NEW WILDCATS

While the East High Class of 2008 are looking forward to college and a bright future, the next generation of Wildcats are waiting in the wings to take their place. They've watched Troy, Gabriella, Sharpay, and the rest of the Wildcats and can't wait to step into their shoes next year!

Jimmie Zara is a basketball ace, just like his hero Troy Bolton. He copies Troy's style and dreams of taking Troy's locker next year.

New Girl

Tiara Gold has just transferred to East High from London, England. She has her sights set on being the next Sharpay!

Sharpay needs a personal assistant to manage her busy senior year schedule. Tiara soon proves that she fits the bill perfectly!

The New Sharpay

Tiara seems to know Sharpay better than Sharpay knows herself. But is the young English rose really as innocent as she seems?

"Hey, good job Troy!"

While everyone congratulates Troy for his clever fake, Donny rushes to celebrate with Jimmie.

Donny Dion
Jimmie's best buddy is Donny Dion. They both dream of being full-fledged Wildcats.

New Hero
In the final moments of the Wildcats' last game, the team is losing. Troy and Coach Bolton have an idea. They put rookie Jimmie Zara in, and while the West High Knights guard Troy, he passes to Jimmie, who makes a winning layup.

GRADUATION

The Wildcats have finally done it! They've put on a great show, graduated high school, and are off to college. It's not always been easy but they've learned a lot, and not just in class! Best of all they have had a great time and made some amazing friends.

Roll Of Honor

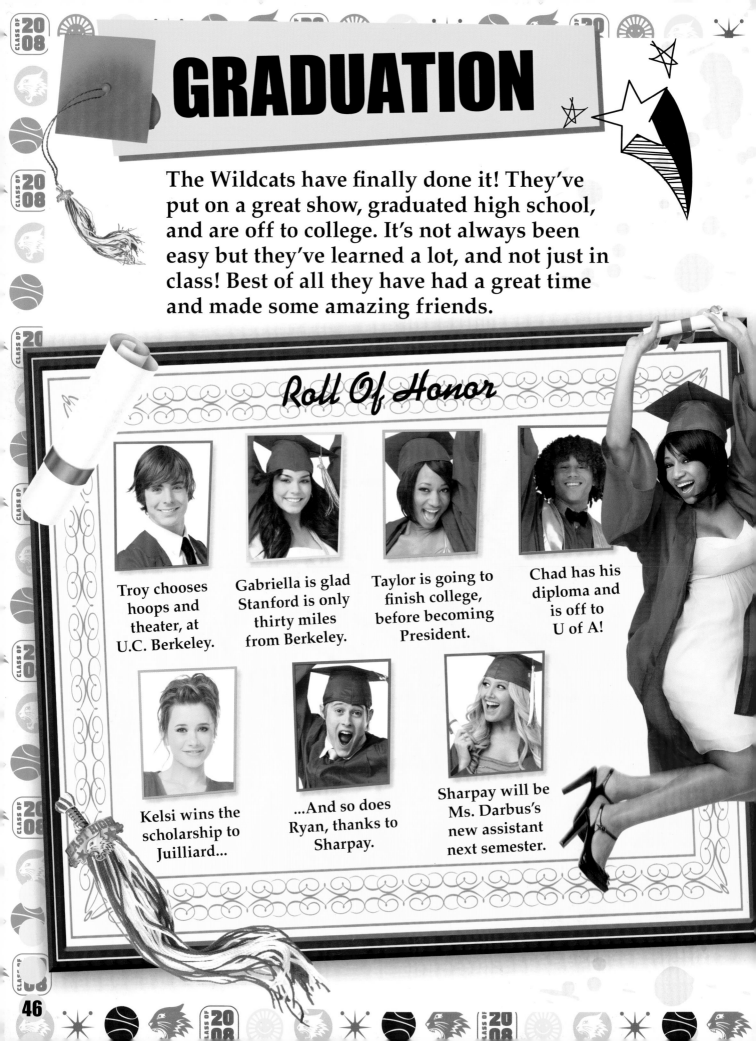

Troy chooses hoops and theater, at U.C. Berkeley.

Gabriella is glad Stanford is only thirty miles from Berkeley.

Taylor is going to finish college, before becoming President.

Chad has his diploma and is off to U of A!

Kelsi wins the scholarship to Juilliard...

...And so does Ryan, thanks to Sharpay.

Sharpay will be Ms. Darbus's new assistant next semester.

Troy and Chad will both play basketball next year, but on different teams!

Troy gives all the way to Stanford to make sure that his first and last dance at East High is with Gabriella.

As the Class of 2008 move on, Tiara, Jimmie, and Donny are ready to take over the halls of East High.

What Team?

At the graduation ceremony for the Class of 2008 Troy Bolton steps up to the podium and speaks for all the Wildcats. They will never forget their time at East High, the things they have learned, or the friends they have made there. After all, "Once a Wildcat, always a Wildcat!"

![Disney]

HIGH SCHOOL MUSICAL

DK

LONDON, NEW YORK, MELBOURNE,
MUNICH, AND DELHI

Designers Lynne Moulding, Lisa Crowe,
Hanna Lāndin, and Owen Bennett
Senior Editor Catherine Saunders
Editorial Assistant Jo Casey
Art Director Lisa Lanzarini
Publishing Manager Simon Beecroft
Category Publisher Alex Allan
Production Editor Sean Daly
Production Controller Amy Bennett

First published in the United States in 2008 by
DK Publishing
375 Hudson Street, New York, New York 10014

First American Edition, 2008
08 09 10 9 8 7 6 5 4 3 2 1

Based on the Disney Channel Original Movie "High School
Musical," Written by Peter Barsocchini
Based on "High School Musical 2," Written by Peter Barsocchini
Based on "High School Musical 3," Written by Peter Barsocchini
Based on Characters Created by Peter Barsocchini

ISBN 978-0-7566-4225-9

Color reproduction by MDP, UK
Printed and bound in the USA by Lake Book Manufacturing, Inc.

Discover more at
www.dk.com